NO LONGER PROPERTY OF
SEATTLE PUBLIC LIBRARY

D0520565

My son, Joe,
first wrote his
version of *The Happy
Book* for his sister, Katie.
I borrowed his title and relied
on his creative help to write this
version. Joe and I dedicate this book
to Katie as well.

VIKING

Penguin Young Readers

An imprint of Penguin Random House LLC

375 Hudson Street · New York, New York 10014

First published in the United States of America by Viking, an imprint of Penguin Random House LLC, 2019

Copyright © 2019 by Andy Rash

Penguin supports copyright. Copyright fuels creativity, encourages diverse voices, promotes free speech, and creates a vibrant culture. Thank you for buying an authorized edition of this book and for complying with copyright laws by not reproducing, scanning, or distributing any part of it in any form without permission. You are supporting writers and allowing Penguin to continue to publish books for every reader.

LIBRARY OF CONGRESS CATALOGING-IN-PUBLICATION DATA IS AVAILABLE.

ISBN 9780451471253

1 3 5 7 9 10 8 6 4 2

Manufactured in China

Welcome to the Happy Book!
I'm one happy Camper!

And I'm happy as a clam!
As a matter of fact, I AM a clam!

Clam
I am

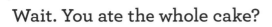

Whee! Hey, is that the end of the book?
That seemed short. Is that a door?
Hey, Clam, come look at this page.

THE SAD BOOK

Oh, hi, Camper. This is where I go when I'm not feeling happy. Meet my friend Trombone.

Bwah-bwah.

I'm just not ready to be in the Happy Book.

THE ANGRY BOOK
Oh, hello, Clam. This is MY new book and MY new friend, Wet Hen.
Bawk bawk bawk!

I'm angry that I can't make you happy and scared we won't be friends anymore.

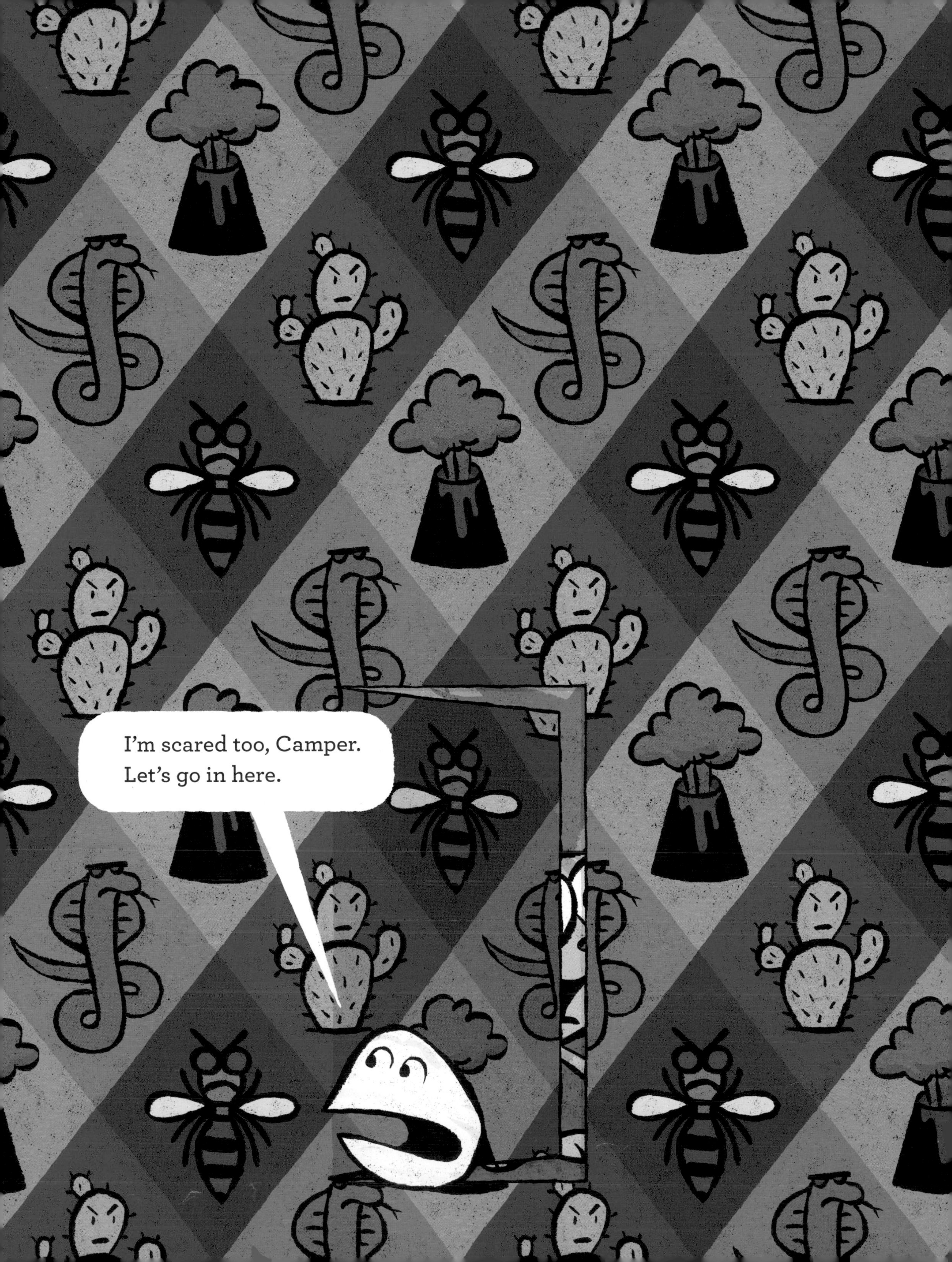
I'm scared too, Camper.
Let's go in here.

KLUNK!
BIKE
But it's not so bad here as long as we're together.
That's how I feel!

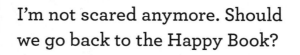

I'm not scared anymore. Should
we go back to the Happy Book?

THE FEELINGS BOOK
Hi, Clam! We're going to have a party! Come on in!

I'm sad the book is almost over.
I'll be angry if I don't get to ride that bike after I worked so hard fixing it after I worked so hard breaking it!
Will there be helmets? I'm scared it might not be safe!

Camper, is this book going to have a happy ending?
As long as we're together, you can feel any way you want about it, pal!